For
Gray
Emily
Luke and
Hannah
(with love)

JANETTA OTTER-BARRY BOOKS

First published in Great Britain in 2012 and in the USA in 2013 by
Frances Lincoln Children's Books, 4 Torriano Mews,
Torriano Avenue, London NW5 2RZ
www.franceslincoln.com

A catalogue record for this book is available from the British Library.

ISBN 978-1-84780-208-8

Illustrated with pastels, watercolour and collage

Set in Mega LT

Printed in Shenzhen, Guangdong, China by C&C Offset Printing in January 2012

1 3 5 7 9 8 6 4 2

Daisy's BIG DIG

ANGIE MORGAN

F

FRANCES LINCOLN
CHILDREN'S BOOKS

I'm Daisy and I live at Number One, Magnolia Street with my mum and dad and Monty, my dog.

I like talking to EVERYONE on our street. But do you think they talk to each other?

No, they don't!

At Number Two lives old Mr Hofmeister.
He's about a hundred and if he had a sign on his door
it would say **KEEP OUT** in big, black, spiky letters.

He has an enormous garden where he grows fantastic
vegetables. Even I eat Mr Hofmeister's vegetables
and I hate vegetables.

At Number Three live the Daves:
Big Dave, Small Dave and Smiley Dave.

They're students so their garden is extremely messy.
Mr Hofmeister calls them rude names. But I like them.

Big Dave helped me with my homework once.
I got a star AND a smiley face.

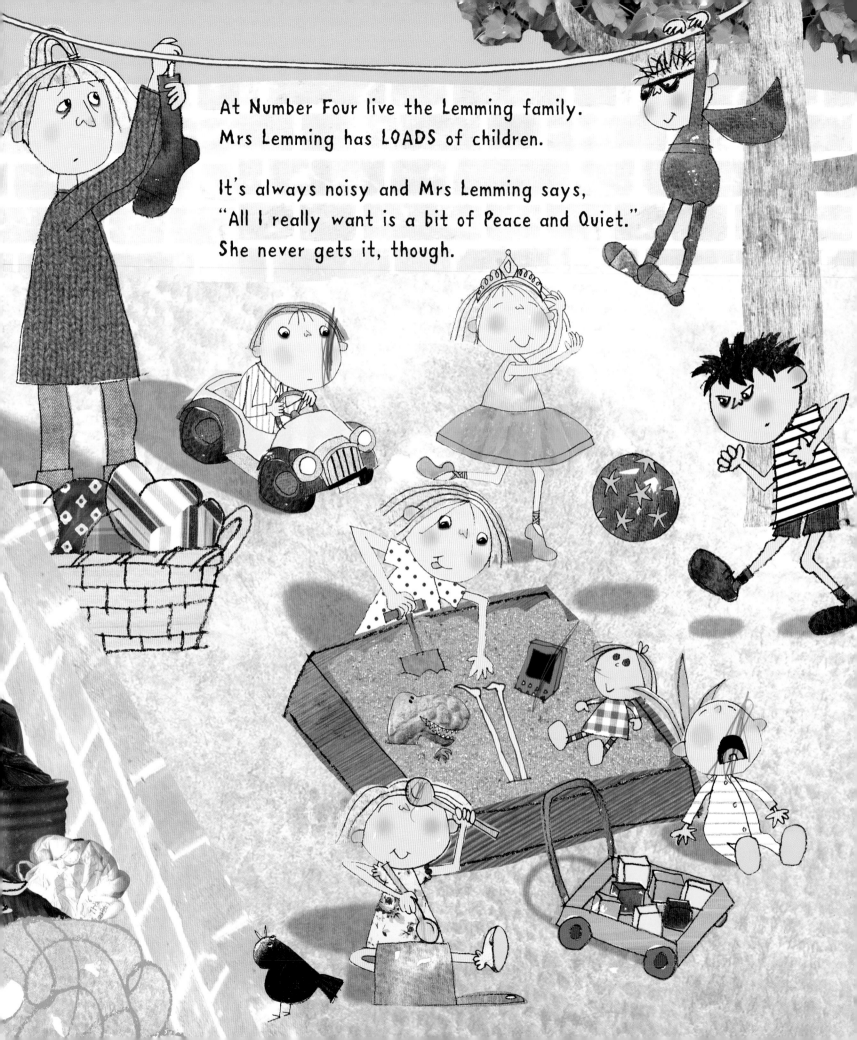

At Number Four live the Lemming family.
Mrs Lemming has LOADS of children.

It's always noisy and Mrs Lemming says,
"All I really want is a bit of Peace and Quiet."
She never gets it, though.

My best friend is Lucy Lemming.
She comes to my house a lot.

She says I'm really lucky to have
a room of my own. She has to share
with her brother, Milo, who picks
his nose and has a tarantula.

At Number Five live Tarquin Fanshawe and his mum and dad.

Tarquin is never allowed out in case he gets dirty or catches something.

He reads all the time and he hasn't even got a TV.

At Number Six lives old Mrs Benjamin.
She makes brilliant cakes and her house always
smells of cooking. She's nearly always smiling
but she sometimes gets sad.

Her daughter and all her grandchildren live in
Australia, which is on the other side of the world.
We've got a globe in our classroom.
That's how I know.

Professor Flowerdew and his wife live next to Mrs Benjamin at Number Seven.

Professor Flowerdew invents things. Once he blew up his shed trying to invent a new kind of electricity.

The fire brigade had to come. It was brilliant.

One day I went round to see old
Mr Hofmeister and he was very worried.
He'd hurt his back lifting a very large
marrow, and now he couldn't dig
his garden.

I wanted to help, so I said, "Don't worry,
Mr Hofmeister. Leave it to me."

I needed a plan,
so I went to find Lucy.

We had a think.

Then we had a snack.

Then we had another think and we came up with a GOOD PLAN.

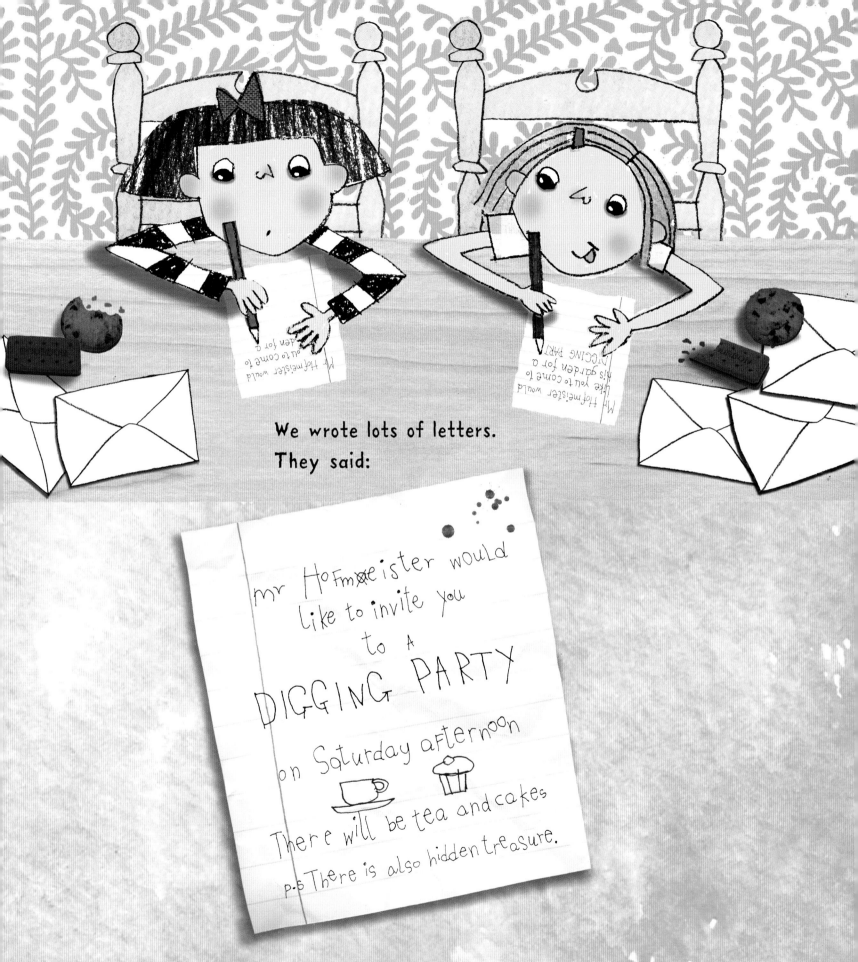

We wrote lots of letters.
They said:

mr Hofmxeister would
like to invite you
to A
DIGGING PARTY
on Saturday afternoon
There will be tea and cakes
p.s There is also hidden treasure.

And then we posted them to all our neighbours.

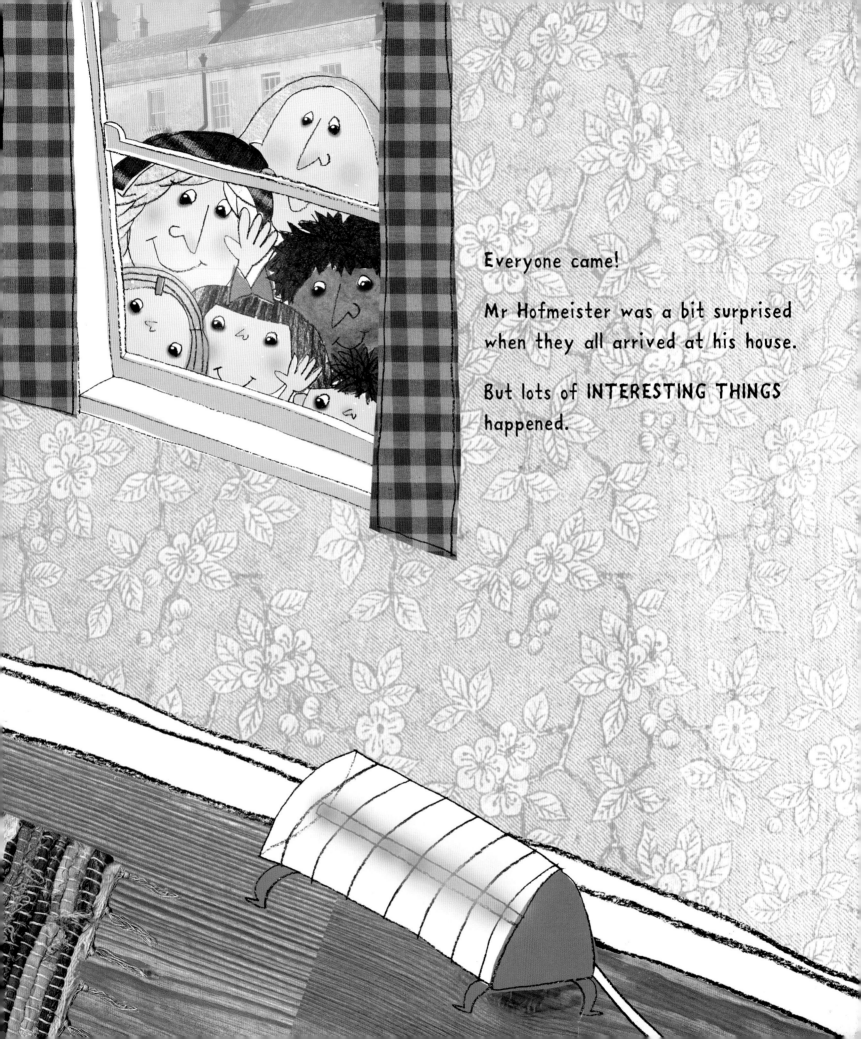

Everyone came!

Mr Hofmeister was a bit surprised when they all arrived at his house.

But lots of INTERESTING THINGS happened.

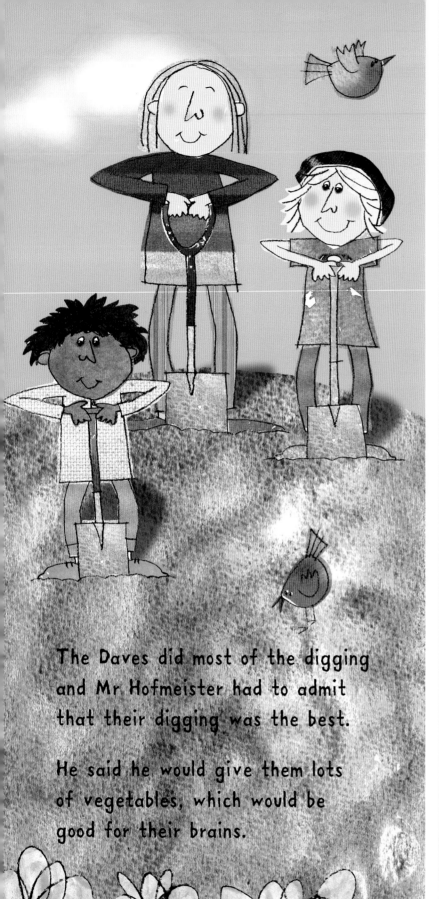

The Daves did most of the digging and Mr. Hofmeister had to admit that their digging was the best.

He said he would give them lots of vegetables, which would be good for their brains.

Tarquin and Professor Flowerdew got on like a shed on fire!

They didn't dig much.

$$x^2 \times y^3 + \left(5 - \frac{9}{23}\right)^3$$

$$4^2 - x(7-4)^3$$

$$\sqrt{895^2}$$

$$\frac{14}{385} \div 72^3 (5-7)^4$$

$$e = mc^2$$

Mrs Benjamin had a really good time digging with the Lemming children.

Mrs Lemming kept saying, "Do let me know if they're a nuisance."

She didn't mean it though. She was enjoying the Peace and Quiet.

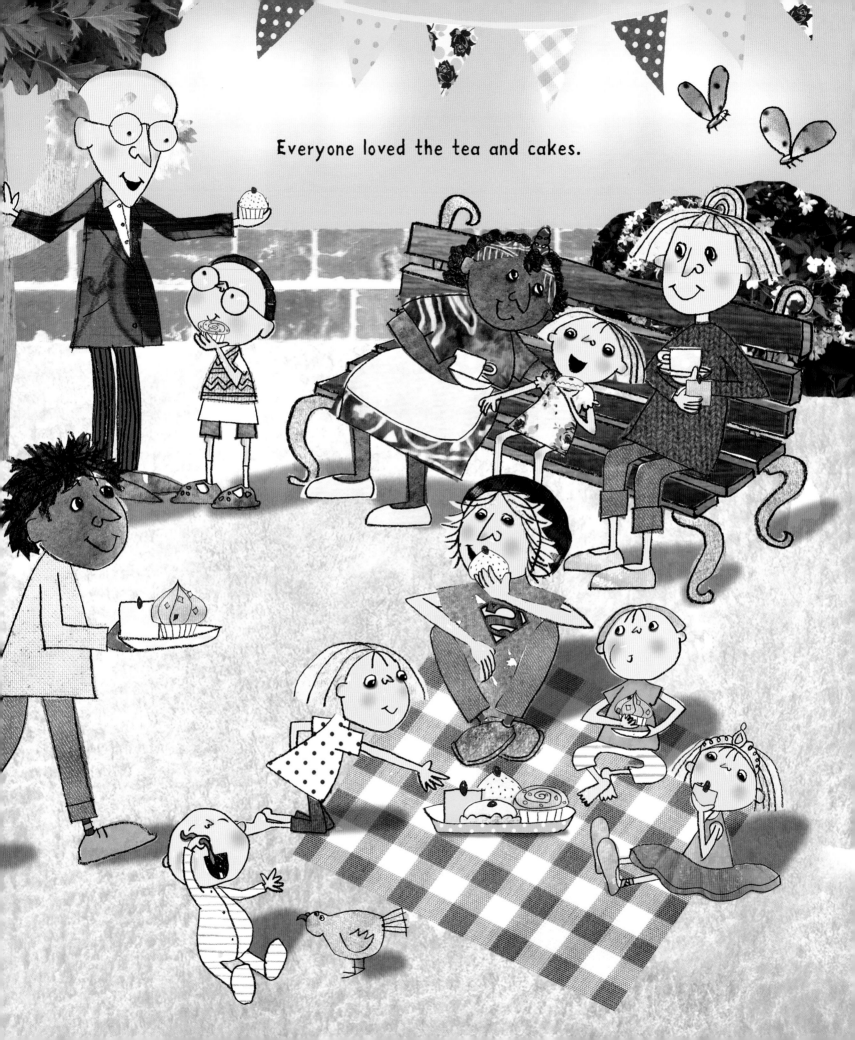

Everyone loved the tea and cakes.

And what happened
after the party?
Well.

Mrs Benjamin had the Lemming children round to her
house a lot and they baked cakes and made things,

and Mrs Lemming FINALLY
got some Peace and Quiet.

Tarquin was able to borrow loads of
interesting books from Professor Flowerdew,
but his mum never let him go in his shed
(just in case of explosions).

Mr Hofmeister and the Daves became good friends, and the Daves did really well at their exams because of eating all those vegetables.

And was there any treasure in Mr Hofmeister's garden?

What do you think?